MY BEAR
I CAN . . . CAN YOU?

My Bear is an irresistible teddy bear
sure to capture the hearts of young readers
and listeners. Each page shows him engaged
in a familiar activity and is accompanied
by a rhyme that is simple, memorable, and
filled with fun. And because every rhyme
ends with a question that calls for
an answer, here is the perfect book for
parents to read with their children!

MY BEAR
I CAN . . . CAN YOU?

Written by Ruth Thomson
Illustrated by Ian Beck

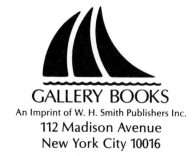

GALLERY BOOKS
An Imprint of W. H. Smith Publishers Inc.
112 Madison Avenue
New York City 10016

I can crack a boiled egg.

I can stand on one leg.
I can reach up and beg. Can you?

I can knock rat-a-tat.

I can let in the cat.

I can wear Grandma's hat.
Can you?

I can count up to ten.
I can point to the hen.

I can build a great den.
Can you?

I can pour my own drink.

I can skate round the rink.

I can give you a wink. Can you?

I can dig in the sand.

I can look very grand.
I can march in the band. Can you?

I can spray with a hose.

I can touch all my toes.
I can wrinkle my nose. Can you?

I can look very tall.
I can walk on a wall.

I can throw a big ball.
Can you?

I can measure my height.

I can ride like a knight.

I can fly my new kite.
Can you?

I can act like a clown.

I can make a gold crown.
I can build a toy town. Can you?

I can sit on a chair.
I can brush my own hair.

I can leap in the air. Can you?

I can tie my own laces.

I can run fast races.

I can make funny faces.
Can you?

First published in 1985 in Great Britain by
Conran Octopus Limited

This edition published in 1990 by Gallery Books,
an imprint of W.H. Smith Publishers, Inc.,
112 Madison Avenue, New York, New York 10016

ISBN 0-8317-6273-X

Designed by Heather Garioch

Printed in Great Britain